Evie,

Always believe
in yourself!

Hope you enjoy the book

Lisa

# Ruby's Secret Gift

Written by Lisa Greenwald
illustrated by Michael LaDuca

ISBN: 978-0-9888714-0-3

Printed in the United States

Inspired by Terry B.

To my amazing husband, Gary,
and my two most precious gifts,
Zachary and Jess.

Ruby Stone woke up with a big smile. She raced downstairs into the kitchen, almost knocking over the glass of orange juice that her mother was handing to Grandma.

"Slow down, Princess Ruby," said Grandma. "Come join us for breakfast."

"I'm so excited," said Ruby. "Today is the Halloween parade at school. I finally get to wear my costume."

Grandma's eyes twinkled as she watched her eight-year-old granddaughter eat a bowl of cereal.

A month ago, Ruby had asked Grandma to help her make a fairytale princess costume for Halloween. It had been so much fun. Grandma and Ruby had gone shopping for the materials and then designed a beautiful dress and crown. Grandma had even taught Ruby how to sew.

Together they had created a magical masterpiece.

Ruby rushed through breakfast, and then made a mad dash for her bedroom. Her red curls bounced with each stride.

Two minutes later, Ruby called down the stairs, "Grandma, would you please help me put on the crown?"

With a soft chuckle, Grandma answered, "Your fairy godmother will be right up!"

Ruby's mother smiled.

Grandma peeked into the bedroom. Ruby stood in the purple gown trimmed with gold lace.

"You look beautiful, young lady," Grandma said.

With tender care, Grandma secured the sparkling crown atop Ruby's red locks. "Now would be the perfect time," thought Grandma.

"I have a special present I want to share with you," Grandma said.

"Really?" asked Ruby.

Ruby saw Grandma's hands hidden deep in the pockets of her old, blue sweater. Ruby wondered if Grandma would pull out a gold locket like the one Heather Grey wore every day to school.

Grandma took her hands from her pockets, but there was no locket. There was nothing. Instead, Grandma gave Ruby one of her big bear hugs.

She whispered softly into Ruby's ear, and as if by magic, Ruby received this very special present.

"Promise me that you will hold onto it forever," Grandma said.

Ruby's eyes filled with wonder. "Thank you, Grandma, I promise I will."

Later that day, the entire school gathered outside to participate in the annual Halloween parade.

This year, Ruby's teacher was Mrs. Hamburger. That was really her name! For the parade, she dressed up like a hot dog. All the children had a good laugh. Even the school principal, Mr. Snicker, cracked a smile when he saw Mrs. Hamburger lead her class past all the families.

Ruby saw her parents and grandmother in the crowd. Grandma winked at her.

Ruby glowed with happiness. She turned to her best friend, Sophie Brilliant. "I truly feel like a fairytale princess," she said. "I love your costume, too. I think it's perfect!"

"Thanks," said Sophie, smiling big.

Sophie was dressed as a bumble-bee, because next week she would be competing in the school spelling bee.

As the two girls followed their class back into the school, Sophie asked, "Ruby, are you excited about the soccer tournament tomorrow?"

"Absolutely!" she replied.

Ruby was happy she would have Grandma's gift with her during the tournament. No one there would see it, not even Sophie.

It was invisible!

The next morning, Ruby and her parents arrived at the soccer field bright and early.

"There's my team!" shouted Ruby, pointing to the Pink Panthers.

Coach Moss called out, "Ruby Stone, don't stand still. Come over here and practice a drill!"

Ruby and her teammates liked it that their coach spoke in rhymes.

Five minutes later, there was the sound of a whistle, and the tournament began.

Over the next few hours, the Pink Panthers would play five different soccer teams.

By late afternoon, the Pink Panthers had played against four teams and won every time. This meant the team was in the final round of the tournament. Now, they would have to play the Green Gazelles for the championship cup.

Coach Moss gathered the Panthers in a circle. All the girls looked a little nervous. To put them at ease, he began with the familiar line, "Girls, I'm Coach Moss. That makes me the boss!"

A few of them giggled. Then there was silence. Skyler Blue burst out, "But Coach, how do we beat the Green Gazelles?"

He answered, "Just pass the ball and run, but make sure you have fun."

So the girls did just that.

With one minute left in the game, the score was tied 3–3.

Skyler quickly passed the ball to Ruby. Ruby was in a position to make a winning goal.

Coach Moss yelled, "You have it, Ruby Stone. Go for the scoring zone!"

Suddenly, Ruby stood frozen in her tracks.

"What if I don't run fast enough?" she thought. "What if I don't kick the ball hard enough? What if I miss the goal?"

As Ruby took a deep breath, she remembered she had Grandma's special gift.

"I'm a strong player," she thought. "I can do this."

With all her might, she kicked the ball into the Green Gazelle's net. Ruby scored the goal to win the championship cup.

The Pink Panthers jumped with joy. In a flash, Ruby's teammate, Scarlett Silver, was at her side. Scarlett was the most popular girl in school.

"Wow, Ruby, you saved the day!" said Scarlett. "Everybody thinks you're the greatest. How about a victory sleepover at my house?"

Ruby was shocked. Scarlett barely spoke to her in school. Now, she was acting like her best friend.

"Uh ... sure," Ruby replied, "just let me ask my parents."

As Ruby ran across the field, she saw her real best friend.

Sophie burst out, "Congratulations, you were amazing! Your parents said we could have a sleepover party."

"Oh no!" thought Ruby, "Who should I choose? Scarlett or Sophie?"

As Ruby wondered what to do, Grandma's gift magically appeared, and the answer became crystal clear. The smart thing to do was to celebrate with her best friend.

Sophie truly cared about Ruby. Scarlett was not a friend at all.

"Sophie, a sleepover sounds great. Just wait right here. There is something I have to do."

Ruby was a little scared. It would take courage to say no to the most popular girl in school. But with Grandma's precious gift, she felt bold. Ruby marched across the field to Miss Popularity.

"Scarlett, thank you for inviting me," she said, "but I want to celebrate with Sophie."

And just like that, Ruby had the strength to walk away. Scarlett stood there, speechless.

Grandma's gift was truly amazing!

That night, Ruby's parents ordered the girls' favorite pizza—meatball and pepperoni. As they ate, the two talked about everything and laughed until there were tears in their eyes.

Suddenly, Sophie became very quiet.

"What's wrong?" asked Ruby.

"I don't think I want to be in the spelling bee anymore," whispered Sophie. "Arthur Wordsly is in the spelling bee, and he's a spelling genius. He won last year's contest. I'm scared I won't stand a chance."

"Nonsense," thought Ruby. Her best friend was really smart. Sophie knew how to spell a lot of hard words. She could even spell the word rhinoceros.

"I won't let you walk away from the contest," exclaimed Ruby.

She knew exactly what Sophie needed. And just like that, Ruby offered her Grandma's magical gift.

Sophie just sat there, deep in thought.

Finally, she smiled, took a deep breath, and said, "I really am good at spelling. I want to challenge Arthur Wordsly in the spelling bee."

On Monday afternoon, everyone was packed into the school auditorium for the spelling bee. Mr. Snicker asked for silence.

All eyes in the audience stared at the twenty boys and girls on stage.

One hour later, there were two students left—Sophie Brilliant and Arthur Wordsly.

Sophie felt brave. No one could see her gift from Ruby, even though she had been using it the whole time.

Mr. Snicker then asked Sophie to spell the word tortoise. Slowly, Sophie uttered the letters, "T-o-r-t-o-s-e."

"That is incorrect," the principal said.

He asked Arthur to spell the same word.

Arthur was silent for a moment. Then, he said, "T-o-r-t-o-i-s-e."

"Correct," Mr. Snicker announced. "Arthur, you are the winner of this year's spelling bee!"

Sophie shook hands with Arthur. Even though she had not won, she had a big smile on her face.

Ruby was not surprised. She knew that, thanks to Grandma's present, Sophie felt like a winner too.

After the contest, school let out. Ruby and Sophie met at their spot by the tree so they could walk home together. Today, their plan was to stop for ice cream cones to celebrate Sophie's good job at the spelling bee.

"Vanilla fudge or chocolate-chip mint?" Ruby asked.

"I think I'll be daring and go for the cookie dough supreme," replied Sophie.

The two girls crossed the school playground, which sat next to the edge of the woods. They saw a few boys from their class standing there, looking down at the ground.

Charlie White looked up and yelled, "Ruby! Sophie! Come look!"

As the girls approached, they heard a faint bark.

The boys were gathered around a small, white puppy wearing a bright pink collar. One of its front paws was caught in a prickly bush.

"When I tried to move the bush, the dog growled," Charlie told the girls.

Ruby whispered to Sophie, "There must be a way we can rescue this poor puppy."

Ruby immediately shut her eyes and put her thinking cap to work.

"I know!" she said finally. "Let's kneel down slowly, so we don't frighten her."

Together, the girls crouched on the ground, and Ruby began humming a lullaby. Sophie chimed in sweetly. The dog's tail wagged happily.

While Ruby gently petted the puppy's back, Sophie carefully lifted the shrub to free its paw. Ruby scooped the trembling animal into her arms.

The puppy licked Ruby's cheek and then Sophie's.

The boys stood there with their mouths wide open.

Charlie gasped. "How did you know what to do?"

At that moment, both girls looked at each other and giggled. They were proud of their newly shared gift.

"Do you think we should tell them?" asked Sophie.

"Yes, we should!" replied Ruby.

Together, the two girls recited Grandma's treasured words: "I have the wisdom, strength, and courage to do it all—because I am a girl."

Then off they went to the police station to report the missing dog. The ice cream cones would wait for another day.